Anna M. Morrison Reed

**The Earlier Poems of Anna M. Morrison**

Anna M. Morrison Reed

**The Earlier Poems of Anna M. Morrison**

ISBN/EAN: 9783337407728

Printed in Europe, USA, Canada, Australia, Japan

Cover: Foto ©Andreas Hilbeck / pixelio.de

More available books at **www.hansebooks.com**

# THE

# EARLIER POEMS

OF

## ANNA M. MORRISON.

---

REVISED AND ARRANGED BY HERSELF.

IN ONE VOLUME.

---

SAN FRANCISCO:

A. L. BANCROFT & CO., PUBLISHERS,

721 MARKET STREET.

1880.

# DEDICATION.

# CONTENTS.

## PART FIRST.

## PART SECOND.

## PART THIRD.

# REQUISITION.

UKIAH, Mendocino Co., Cal.,
November 11, 1878.

MRS. ANNA M. REED,

*Dear Madam :*

We scarcely need to apologize for the request we are about to make. We watched your course with much pleasure during your girlhood, at the time when you were edifying and enlightening the public with your pleasing and able lectures, for which the people always expressed their highest appreciation, both publicly and privately.

And now, having learned that you are about to prepare another treat for us, in the nature of a volume of poems:

We earnestly request, that you publish it at an early day, feeling certain that the appearance of the volume—the production of one of California's own—will receive the hearty approbation of, and be welcomed by, the public.

With great esteem,

We are yours very truly,

R. McGARVEY,
THOMAS L. CAROTHERS,
J. H. DONOHOE,
SAM. WHEELER,
J. H. SEAWELL,
ALEX. MONTGOMERY.
J. L. WILSON,
JAMES FOWZER,
W. W. CUNNINGHAM,
G. B. MATHERS,
Rev. J. D. SHERIDAN,
E. W. KING.
A. O. CARPENTER.

SANTA ROSA:
BARCLAY HENLY,
J. K. LUTTRELL.

SACRAMENTO:
WILLIAM IRWIN,
WM. H. MILLS,
N. GREENE CURTIS,
S. C. DENSON.

BERKELEY:
Very Rev. P. M. COMERFORD,
M. C. O'TOOLE, M. D.

SAN FRANCISCO:

✚ J. S. ALEMANY,
Archbishop, S. F.
Bro. JUSTIN,
President Christian Brothers.
GEO. PEN. JOHNSTON,
OGDEN HOFFMAN,
WILLIAM ALVORD,
J. P. HOGE,
WM. T. WALLACE,
P. J. THOMAS,
JAS. R. KELLY,
ROBERT F. MORRISON,
WM. H. L. BARNES,
HALL McALLISTER,
S. M. WILSON,
GEORGE C. PERKINS,
H. F. PAGE.

MARYSVILLE:

Right Rev. EUGENE O'CONNELL,
Rev. T. GRACE,
Rev. T. NUGENT,
Rev. T. KIRLEY,
NICHOLAS GAFFORD,

J. SMYTHE,
M. E. CASEY,
W. FITZGERALD,
P. CORCORAN,
SISTERS OF NOTRE DAME,
P. L. BUNCE,
D. KERTCHEM,
T. O'REILLEY,
G. HARNEY,
J. BROGAN,
T. POWERS,
E. CARMODY,
M. KERNS,
P. McGINNIS,
P. C. SLATTERY,
Father BUHOLZER,
M. McADAMS.

SMARTSVILLE:

Rev. M. COLEMAN,
ANNIE COLEMAN,
JOSIE O'BRIEN,
AGNES COLEMAN.

CHICO:

JOHN BIDWELL.

# PREFACE.

In the foregoing invitation the reader will find my best excuse for publishing this collection of writings. With the exception of a very few, the signers have known me and my history since childhood.

The poems included in the volume, with the exception of perhaps a dozen, were composed between the ages of ten and twenty.

And of those passing judgment upon my work I ask but this—*to remember the circumstances under which it was done.*

For *writing*, I make no apology. The good, the true, the beautiful have spoken to my heart, and shown me some of the divine things in God's grand creation ; the wondrous light from those sources of inspiration has fallen o'er me, and I have paused within its radiance, my soul so filled with sunshine that, with eyes dazzled and downcast, I have dared to sing my simple songs about them, not knowing *why* I sang.

If the themes be old, perhaps the melodies are sweet. The lark's song is a most familiar thing, yet words have never told its burden of glad meaning. A winged voice, it rises from the dull earth to the brilliant sky. We listen with an upturned face and eager heart. And with its echo comes the spell of long-lost springs, the dreams of faded summers, and the reveries of vanished autumns. It is ever new, ever sweet in its suggestive melody, and yet the notes are *old*—unchanged since time began.

So a pure thought happily spoken—a truth sweetly and gracefully expressed—though it has been spoken or written a thousand times, may suggest a hope, a recollection, or a *better thought,* and lift a once-despairing face toward a fairer sky.

The *best* we can expect in music, art, or literature is the suggestion of something *better.* The artist, when he looks upon his handiwork, dreams of something *nearer* his ideal, that his busy brain may yet conceive and his obedient fingers execute. The composer, with the notes of his masterpiece ringing in his ears, hears in fancy the grander theme *this* melody suggests. The author, excelling in verse and brilliant periods, sees *still beyond* him his best and purest inspiration. Not *here* is found perfection, nor until upon the troubled soul of each child of genius, Divinity has written peace. Then why should I, in bringing this, the first offering of my early years, crave pardon for its many deficiencies?

To those who have invited this publication I do return my heartfelt gratitude; because among them are numbered those whose encouragement and appreciation have long brightened and blest my life. And for their sake, and in consideration of the compliment they have paid me, I hope that my book will not fall below the expectation of the public.

And since its sale will effect, in a measure, the welfare of some near and dear to me, and the completion of my efforts in their behalf (though its financial fate is immaterial to myself), I pray for its success, and, with the faith that has ever sustained me, cast my bread upon the waters, knowing that it will return to me "after many days."

A. M. M.

# NOTE BY THE AUTHOR.

The following life sketch was written by the late John C. McPherson. Its truth, brevity, and literary excellence will commend it to the readers of this volume.

Its gifted but eccentric author was well known to the newspaper fraternity and literary people of this coast. And despite his peculiarities, in his death our world of letters has met with an irreparable loss, as has also the State; for few men in California were as well acquainted with her history and the biography of her early pioneers.

There are many to-day in the State who have been benefited by the labor of his brain and pen; and I herewith subscribe twenty-five dollars toward securing a fitting monument,to place above him, where he lies in his unmarked grave in Stanislaus. I appeal to the editors and private individuals who have known him and his writings, asking that *they* also contribute something to his memory, and trust that my suggestion may meet with a just response.

All wishing to communicate with me upon the subject will address me at Ukiah, Mendocino county, Cal.

ANNA M. REED.

*February*, 1880.

# ANNA M. MORRISON.

In recent peregrinations through a portion of Yuba County, we had the great pleasure of forming the acquaintance of the beautiful and gifted young lady whose name stands above, and also the gratification of hearing her lecture in the theater at Timbuctoo, her subject being, "Woman, her Rights and Proper Spheres of Action." Before speaking of her lecture we trust that a brief biographical sketch of her young life may not be deemed uninteresting.

Miss Morrison was born in the city of Dubuque, in the State of Iowa, and is the eldest living child of Guy B. and Mary E. Morrison. At the time of her birth her father was engaged in merchandising, and was in affluent circumstances; but meeting with reverses, he came at an early day to California, and engaged in mining in Butte County. He had left his wife and Anna, the latter then an infant, in the care of Mr. S. B. Preston, her grandfather on the maternal side. This gentleman was a member of the Society of Friends, of fine intellect, and one of the best chemists in the United States at the time. Mr. Preston was a native, we believe, of Baltimore, from which city, and some time after he had completed his education, he went west, and resided some time in Illinois, also in Wisconsin, and at last died at Dubuque, leaving behind him a character of unsullied purity, of private worth, and inflexible integrity.

The grandfather of Miss Anna, on the paternal side, is the venerable Mr. Jesse Morrison, at one time of Kaskaskia, subsequently, and for many years, and still, a resident of Galena, Illinois. This gentleman is now in his eighty-fifth year, and, from recent advices, is hale and hearty, and in full possession of his mental faculties, always said to be of a high order, and is honored and esteemed by the community where he resides. His long life has been characterized by a disinterested devotion to the interests of noble and humane objects, and when he will go to the grave, he will be accompanied by the regret and lamentations of thousands. (This aged good man was the uncle of your distinguished fellow-citizen, Hon. Robert F. Morrison, Chief Justice of the Supreme Court of this State; also, of the gallant soldier, farmer, and statesman of the west, Gen. William R. Morrison.)

In 1854, when but a mere child, the subject of our sketch, accompanied by her mother, came to California, by way of Panama, and found her father at Oregon City, a small mining camp, six miles north of Oroville, in Butte County.

There for ten years she resided with her parents, her father being engaged in mining. Without the advantage of schools or society, and with no companions, save those which home and books afforded, the early years of Anna's life passed away. At the young age of ten, her taste for writing displayed itself. In 1864, the family moved to a farm in the vicinity of Wyandotte, another small mining town, six or seven east of Oroville.

The first of her productions which appeared in print, and which she transmitted, doubtless with fear and trembling, to the San Francisco press, was a poem entitled "Our Nation's Prayer." This was in the fall of 1864, when she was yet but a little girl.

In January, 1868, Anna, with her parents, three little brothers, and sister, moved to Dunham Farm, Oroville.

Always thirsty for knowledge, the heroic young girl at last, partly through her own exertions, and partly through the influence of two respected gentlemen, Dr. C. S. Haswell, and his son-in-law, Mr. Wm. H. Mills, of Sacramento, secured admittance, in July, 1868, to Mrs. Perry's Seminary, in Sacramento City, and attended that excellent institution, in company with Miss Emma Haswell, as a day scholar, and boarded in the family of the worthy doctor.

She assiduously applied herself to her studies, but unfortunately, in a little over two months, received a dispatch, calling her home to Oroville on account of sickness in her father's family.

She immediately returned on the first of October, following the July she had entered school, to find her people sick and helpless, utterly worn down by chills and fever· Anna was the only member of the family strong and in good health.

Her father was out of money and in debt, and immediately following the instincts of her nature, she exerted herself for the relief of those so near and dear to her. She prepared some essays, and on the evening of the twentieth of October, 1868, delivered he first lecture to a crowded house, at Tehama, in Tehama County.

Since the commencement of her public career, she has always, and most deservedly, been financially and otherwise successful.

The mother of this "child of nature," this "Butte County girl," as the *Butte Record* and hundreds of both sexes in that county delight to call her, was reared in ease and refinement, and received a first-class education in the city of Baltimore. When convalescing from sickness, and the whole family was steeped in drear adversity, she would take a pan, pick, and shovel, and, accompanied by her little, eldest boy, extract some gold from auriferous earth, and thus, by her exertions, this lady of culture and education was enabled to keep the " wolf from the door."

But her devoted daughter was soon enabled to afford relief.

The receipts attending her lectures were, after paying personal expenses, always remitted to her parents, and at length, on the twelfth day of March, 1869, she removed the whole family, yet weak and worn from sickness, from the scenes of their sorrows and misfortunes to a place in the vicinity of Timbuctoo, in Yuba County, which she had secured for them, and formerly belonging to Judge O. F. Redfield.

Since moving to this place, Anna has traveled and lectured, always accompanied by one of her brothers, younger than herself, in the counties of Nevada, Placer, El Dorado, Amador, Calaveras, Colusa, Tehama, Shasta, Trinity, Siskiyou, Klamath, Butte, Plumas, Sierra, and Yuba. And everywhere meeting with great success.

The press, that great lever of public opinion, has been loud in its commendation of her ability as a lecturer.

Such, then, is a brief sketch of the young life of Miss Anna M. Morrison, and true to the letter, and we confidently hope that no one who has not an adamantine heart, will read our simple relation of the story of her youthful years, her sufferings and privations, the disadvantages she labored under from the want of a scholastic education and culture, her filial devotion, her exertions for the relief of her kindred when she was but a little girl, the nobility and heroism of her soul, the untarnished purity of her worth, pure as the snow-flakes now falling on the glistening peaks of the Sierra Nevadas—we say that no one, surely, but with the most obdurate, adamantine heart, will fail to appreciate this good young girl, and say earnestly: "God speed her."

Altogether, she has never been to school more than twelve months, and remembering this, with other early disadvantages, this gifted child of nature, as is often said, is an honor to her sex.

Her lecture, referred to in the first part of this sketch, was an able one, not only in our estimation, but of every one who heard it. She is opposed to woman's "right of suffrage," but pointed out in forcible language, and, as we thought, by incontrovertible argument, numerous avenues leading to distinction, for women to walk, which would not interfere with high and holy duties pertaining to domestic life, which the right to vote would by no means contribute to improve, but detract from the sacredness of woman's true sphere on earth, which is to make home happy, and to the best of her ability ameliorate the condition of suffering humanity.

Without expressing an opinion on the propriety or impropriety of the right of woman to vote, we can only say that Miss Morrison is sincere and earnest in her convictions, and sustains them with great ability. She must be heard to be appreciated.

To those who have not seen her, we can only describe her as a beautiful young lady, with cheeks like the petals of a rose, with a sparkling, loving, dark-brown eye, beaming with intelligence, and rich, dark-brown hair. Her enunciation is clear, distinct, and melodious; her language elegant and forcible; her smile winning and fascinating; and her whole life characterized by a noble devotion and true morality.

We predict for Miss Anna M. Morrison a bright and prosperous future, and a just appreciation of her intellectual ability and true character.

JOHN C. McPHERSON.

I have been happy, and the light
  From vanished days falls gently through
The rifts between the darker ones
  That cloud my heaven's glorious blue.
I have been happy, and apart,
  To-day, from that familiar time,
The bird-songs echo in my heart,
  And sweet the "bells of mem'ry" chime.

Happy I am, though faded fields
  Lie where the spring flowers used to bloom;
Happy I am, although my feet          .
  Have paused by many a loved one's tomb.
The promise of life's early morn
  Old Time has kept right well for me,
And in the passing years I read
  Fulfillment of that prophecy.

I will be happy when the past
  Upon the future shuts the gate,
When all my transient hopes are o'er,
  And I can only "stand and wait,"
Singing, my soul will bow before
  The chastening of the mystic rod,
And on the wings of gladness go
  Forth to the summons of its God.

# PART FIRST.

POEMS COMPOSED BETWEEN THE AGES OF TEN AND
FIFTEEN YEARS.

## DREAMING AMONG THE FLOWERS.

Gathering wild flowers from the hillside,
    How each modest gem I prize,
Wondering, will I ever gather
    Flowers from fields in Paradise?

Wondering, will I pass o'er safely
    The narrow path my Savior trod?
And across the silent river
    Dwell forever with my God.

As from my heart that hope is stealing,
    Upward through the summer air,
I think the angels surely hear it,
    Though it forms no worded prayer.

They always know the soul's devotion,
    Patient suff'ring makes more pure,
And oftentimes our lives are better
    For the trials we endure.

This dreaming day-dreams in the sunshine
    Grows still dearer to my heart,
Although it seems to others childish,
    Of *my life* it is a part.

Oh, will I ever quite forget it?
 Or this love for gath'ring flowers?
While thinking can they be much fairer,
 Those that bloom in heaven's bowers?

Flowers with eyes of blue and amber,
 Blooming in the fields of green;
Where the murmuring streams of crystal
 Gleam like bands of silver sheen;

I wonder, will I taste those waters?
 And find rest the world denies,
Gathering white and fragrant lilies
 In the fields of Paradise?


## THE NATION'S PRAYER.

God of the true, the brave and free,
A prayer ascends from earth to thee,
It comes from the north far, far away;
'Tis heard where southern brooklets play.

It is one united, wailing cry,
Suing for mercy from on high.
Wilt thou not pity, hear, and heed
A nation's prayer, in this great need?

Can aught appease or stay thy wrath?
O Jesus! plead in our behalf;
In pity turn a listening ear,
Our agony's petition hear.

Free our land from this scourge of sin,
And let it be what it has been;
Lift thou the cloud from our country's fame,
Let dove-eyed Peace be queen again.

Oh! surely 'twill thy pity move
To grant us mercy from above;
To see, deluged with blood and pain,
Our glorious Union cleft in twain.

## LINES

COMPOSED WHEN THE AUTHORESS WAS IN HER ELEVENTH YEAR.

Little flower so pure and sweet,
Lowly bending at my feet,
I will listen for a while
To thy teachings free from guile.

Little flower with starry eye
Looking upward to the sky,
Softly thou doth seem to say:
"Look, like me, from earth away."

Little flower of brightest blue,
I take thee, wet with sparkling dew,
From the breast of Mother Earth,
To adorn my lonely hearth.

Little flower so dear to me,
A lesson I have learned from thee
To give my all, and humbly find
The task Christ has to me assigned.

Little flower, I bless the day
That led my wand'ring feet this way;
An angel in disguise thou art,
Whispering to my lonely heart.

## "THE TENDER GRACE OF A DAY THAT IS DEAD."

I dream of the summer lost and dead,
  Of the charm of the words then spoken,
Before the "silver cord" was loosed,
  And the "golden bowl" was broken.

Each dreary day, at the window low,
  I list to the restless winds sighing,
Watching the faded leaves whirl to rest;
  Beneath them I wish I was lying.

Wond'ring, they ask why, these autumn days,
  I watch the dead leaves while they're falling—
Like my summer hopes they seem to me,
  To the peace of the grave seem calling.

The silver cord of love is loosed,
  And faith's golden bowl at last broken;
The charms of life are forever gone,
  Like the fond words that once were spoken.

And 'twere better if my days were spent
  With the summer mournfully ended;
For the autumn winds, and falling leaves,
  And my life, seem strangely blended.


## JESSE'S GRAVE.

Out on the hillside, where the last lingering ray
Of sunlight falls at the close of day,
They have laid him to rest, and left us to weep,
In the morning of life he has fallen asleep.

As onward we journey, amidst care and sin,
When the present is dark, and the future is dim,
How our hearts will turn fondly in silence and tears,
To the grave on the hillside, as year succeeds years.

But sorrow not those who in youth depart,
Whispers a voice in our inmost heart;
For after the day comes the night with its gloom,
And the pathways of life all lead to the tomb.

So we pray, when this pilgrimage is at last done,
We also may rest where the rays of the sun
So tenderly fall at the close of the day,
While our spirits, with his, rejoice far away.


## AT TWILIGHT—SUMMERTIME.

Winds so gently stealing round my woodland bower,
Hush me to oblivion of life one little hour.
Busy brain, cease toiling, striving e'er to gaze
From the present darkness through the future's haze.

Why this tearful waiting, why not be at rest,
Free from care and sorrow, on dear nature's breast?
Do not chide my longing thus to lie asleep,
Where, at least, the blossoms over me would weep.

Grows my heart so weary, what have I to cheer?
Is it strange that often falls the burning tear?
And my young life, saddened by its weight of care,
Learns to love the twilight's tender hour of prayer?

Then winds, so gently sighing, linger in your stay,
With your soft caresses steal my life away;
Father of all, in mercy, pity one so lone,
Angels in the twilight, bear my spirit home.

## LOST.

Pure no more, and no more true,
　Thou art a ruined heart, poor Angeline!
What to me is earthly love?
　*Thine* for *me* did not endure, Angeline.

The glance of thy winning eye
　Held me once in bondage sweet, Angeline;
And still, though that power is past,
　My worn heart grieves over thee, Angeline.

*So* gladly I'd see thee lie
　Down to thy last long sleep, loved Angeline,
If thou couldst but wake again
　Pure in another world—O, Angeline!

Lost to heaven, perchance, and me,
　False as thy false vows, tempted Angeline,
I pray now that nevermore
　Thy fair face I'll see, fallen Angeline.

True no more, and no more pure,
　Thou art a ruined heart, lost Angeline;
Love, I know, can not endure,
　Thine was *false*, and mine *betrayed*, Angeline.


## RESURRECTION.

Under the snow lies the lily and rose,
　Far to the south the swallow has flown,
Summer's asleep with her beautiful flowers,
　In a grave where the winter winds moan.

Cold in the tomb lie the ones we have loved,
　Gone are the dreams of vanishing youth,
The winter of care is chilling our hearts,
　Blighting the flowers of love and of truth.

*Wait*—spring will come with her sunshine and warmth,
  Soon back o'er the wave the swallow will fly,
Summer will waken to music and bloom,
  To be wooed by the zephyr's soft sigh.

*Hope*—from the tomb the souls we have loved
  Fly to some beautiful harbor of rest,
*Real* are the dreams we have cherished so long,
  Winter and sorrow, unknown to the blest.


## OUT IN THE WIND AND THE RAIN.

The night's dark and wild, and its voices to me
  Seem wailing a weird and mystic refrain;
My heart throbs with woe as I start from my rest,
  For my darling lies out in the wind and the rain.

I wept yester eve till I sank to my sleep,
  And dreamed you were living, and loved me again;
But the wrath of the storm is chilling my soul,
  For I know you are cold in the wind and the rain.

You went to your rest in the beautiful May;
  I knew you were safe from all trial and pain;
I could bear that you slept 'neath the blossoms of spring,
  But oh! not alone, in the wind and the rain.

'Neath the tree where you sleep, through the long summer
    day,
  Pond'ring over the past, on the grass I have lain—
But now *I* am sheltered away from the storm,
  While you'll never come in from the wind and the rain.

But there will come an hour, when the last trump shall wail
  O'er the graves of the dead, to awake them again;
Then no more will the tomb hold the form that I love,
  No more will I weep at the wind and the rain.

## A PAGE FROM LIFE.

The sky is dark, with wind and storm
  The branches drip against the wall,
But not in keeping with the night
  The brilliance of the banquet-hall.

Above the sighing of the rain,
  Swell sounds of flute and violin
That time to mazes of the waltz
  The tread of feet that stray in sin.

Here haste the heedless human throng,
  To grasp the follies as they go,
Forgetting that in songs of earth
  There wakes an undertone of woe.

Here smiles the maid, as to her lips
  Mad Pleasure holds her sparkling bowl;
She does not see the dregs below,
  Where waits the ruin of her soul.

Here comes the man who, proud and young,
  Yet drinks from out the baleful cup,
Nor heeds the serpent coiled beneath
  The beaded wine that fills it up.

He tramples o'er a fond wife's trust,
  Who weeps to see his downward course;
Her fresh young heart he idly won
  To fill her life with love's remorse.

But still with him, in merry throngs,
  She seeks in vain her grief to hide;
But wounded to the death is love,
  And dying is her hope and pride.

In scenes like this, in other days,
　　Contentment sang her songs to me;
But hushed her voice of quiet joy,
　　And now they seem a mockery.

Perhaps my eyes are wiser now,
　　And pierce the vail of poor deceit
That once could hide the weariness
　　Of hearts that followed noisy feet.

\*　　\*　　\*　　\*　　\*

But hush! they play a tune I've loved;
　　It wakes my soul to wild desire
To live the life I *once* have lived—
　　The music thrills like liquid fire.

I seem to stand within a room,
　　Upon an eve that long since fled;
I hear the hum, I see the glare,
　　Of voice and light now still and dead.

I turn to greet your tender eyes,
　　For on these waves of melody
Comes back again the only voice
　　That spoke but loving words to me.

O Death! that voice is still beneath
　　Your chilling breath—and oh! so cold
Have grown the hands that folded lie
　　Beneath the graveyard's dreadful mold.

I am alone—I find no more
　　Such love as blessed my early youth—
Light rest the sod above the heart,
　　That was all purity and truth.

\*　　\*　　\*　　\*　　\*　　\*

The banquet o'er, into the night
  The human tide ebbs from the hall,
The lights have almost faded out,
  And darkness deepens like a pall.

As wearied dancers seek their homes,
  I follow slowly their retreat—
The storm still lingers o'er the town,
  And pools of water fill the street.

I sit within my room and dream
  Of all the strange wants of my life—
My sorrow is so sad and deep,
  And crueler than pain or strife.

My place is not in joyful throngs,
  That with their songs and merry scenes
Recall to me the vanished past,
  And that lost face that haunts my dreams.


### AFTER SUNSET.

Softly falls upon the hills,
  The sable shade of evening's wing.
And the bright star in the west
  Proves the night is closing in.

As the amber of the clouds
  Faded into silver-gray,
So the light of every life
  Fades at last from earth away.

So must sink the sun of life,
  So the night of Death must fall,
And the shadow of his wing
  Soon or late must rest on all.

Hushed the cooing of the dove
　　Seeking in the pine repose,
And the south wind's gentle breath
　　Folds the petals of the rose.

So the petals of our trust
　　Fold around the heart we love,
Though the chill of sorrow's breath
　　Makes us silent like the dove.

## "LEAD US NOT INTO TEMPTATION."

Sweet with the sweetness of noxious fruit—
　　Fair with the charm of a siren's smile,
Sin ever holds but remorse in store,
　　But not the less does its spell beguile.

It steals like perfume from a poison flower,
　　To lull the sense and to chill the heart;
It shines beyond, like the miraged bourne,
　　That, as we follow, does still depart.

Its memory comes like a spice wind, blown
　　Through a dread sirocco, that blasts and sears
Till the spirit faints in the laden heat
　　That dries, too oft, the repentant's tears.

Shun, O my heart! the wildering ways,
　　Where the flower and smile prove the wanderer's
　　　bane;
For the "gathered rose" is a gathered thorn,
　　And the "stolen sweet" but a stolen pain.

## TO A FRIEND.

Out in the balmy sunlight
   To utter a last "good-by,"
On a morning long ago,
   We were standing, you and I.

And as bright as the sunshine
   Were the hopes of my young life;
I knew not then of sorrow,
   Or the world's rude wear and strife.

The spot where we stood that summer
   Does not look the same to-day,
Each year has brought it changes,
   The old tree is cut away.

Yet dear is the place as ever,
   And while tracing life's lone track
I shut my eyes and wonder
   If that time will not come back.

But no; on life's broad ocean
   You have drifted far from me,
Perhaps you have forgotten
   The hillside and the tree.

But you I never can forget,
   And as the years go by,
Upon the sloping hillside
   They will lay me when I die.

And when I there am sleeping
   On some future summer day,
Fate some time may bring you back,
   To the hillside you may stray.

As you linger on the by-path,
    May your wandering feet be led
To the spot where I am resting
    In my quiet, lowly bed.

Then stoop for me and gather
    One little flower of blue,
And keep it in remembrance
    Of the heart to friendship true.


## HANNAH.

Down where the willows sweep
    Their trailing branches to the summer air,
Where tender blossoms weep,
    They laid my little friend, so young and fair.

Where gentle breezes bring
    The sweetest perfume from the flowering hill,
Where birds incessant sing,                          ·
    She sleeps, her loving voice forever still.

There the water-lily trails
    Its waxen leaves upon the crystal tide,
And there my heart bewails
    That years ago my little playmate died.

And often now I dream
    Of Hannah, with the eyes so sad and brown;
The while from some bright world,
    Perhaps upon me she is looking down.

## SONG.

You may not miss me, darling,
  While the tide of life is strong,
While *your* world holds yet its pleasure
  In a round of dance and song.

And I know you will not miss me
  When the loving gather round,
And by soft, impassioned glances,
  Your truant heart is bound.

But when the world is fading,
  And time has marked your brow,
You will sadly, sadly miss me,
  Although you do not now.

Too well will you remember
  The hand that once caressed,
And eyes whose lingering glances
  Love's tenderness confessed.

Perhaps in some far country,
  In life's sad afternoon,
You'll dream about its morning
  That passed away so soon.

And there among the shadows,
  There will come a gentle tread,
And some voice we knew together
  Will tell you I am dead.

And with your retrospection
  Will come a wild regret,
For all our past, my darling,
  *You never can forget.*

## AT THE SCHOOL-HOUSE PINE.

I have wandered to-day to the old pine tree,
   Where we used to laugh together;
The pleasures of life seem over for me,
   And their charm is lost forever.

And sitting beneath the grieving boughs,
   I think of the days departed,
And smile through tears to remember the cause
   That's making me broken-hearted;

And I say, though you know not what it is,
   Of the world I'm sadly weary;
For my childhood's faith in life is lost,
   And the future looks so dreary.

So I can not help but grieve to day,
   Where we used to laugh together;
For the pleasures of life are over for me,
   And their charm seems lost forever.

## A PICTURE.

The night-winds moan across the barren moor,
   The pale moon struggles through a misty vail,
And smoky vapors rolling from the sea,
   Come burdened with the ground-owl's mournful wail.

Upon the drearest spot of all the waste
   Stands a lone tree, whose branches gnarled and old,
Wind-rocked and mutt'ring, seem to ever grieve
   O'er burden of some mystery they hold.

No pen can paint the scene, so desolate,
   The weird, unearthly bearing of the night—
Fit place it seems for tragedy and death,
   The heart shrinks, shuddering, at the ghostly sight.

East from the tree, across the pallid waste,
  Upon a spot that forms almost a knoll,
Stands an old house in ruin and decay,
  Fit haunt it seems for some poor, wandering soul.

And sure 'tis said, by those who know the place,
  On Indian summer nights are heard and seen
Strange voices and strange sights, that flit around
  Like the fantastic phantoms of a dream.

Near by the house, upon the eastern slope,
  Unmarked, save by a cross, two graves were found;
No mourner ever comes to tend or care,
  Or drop a tear upon the lonely mound.

Oft have I wandered o'er the haunted moor,
  And puzzled o'er the mystery it holds,
While sadly rose the killdees' weeping cry
  From marshy flats that edge the dry, bare wolds.

But still unanswered may I ever roam,
  While over all the bleak winds sigh and rave;
For nevermore to mortal ear will come
  A voice from out the portals of the grave.


## MUSINGS IN THE WANE OF SUMMER.

### I.

The summer droops to autumn's arms,
  Our Californian hills are bright
  With gorgeous dyes and purple light—
Our land seems free from all alarms.
The farms that nestle 'mong the hills
  Are fully fraught with fruit and grain,
  Of kine there comes a low refrain,
In harmony chime birds and rills.

Across the fields of ripened wheat
  The speckled quail in gladness pipe;
  The larks their swelling joys recite,
And, full-mouthed, fly their young to meet.

It seems all nature stops to thank,
  In melody, the master hand
  That strews with blessings all the land,
From human life to herbage rank.

I gaze with smiling eyes across
  The landscape to the earth's blue rim—
  There comes a thought—my eyes are dim
With consciousness of one great loss.

Still, should I damp this joy with tears,
  And make a discord with my moan,
  Because my trust in life has flown,
And left me sad, with trembling fears?

No, let them sing their carols sweet,
  Until the harvest-moon is dead,
  And silent all the song and tread
Of thankful voice and hurried feet.

Then, when the autumn days grow dark,
  And all the land's awatch for rain,
  I low will chant my grieving strain,
Without reproof from man or lark.

### II.

The day is drawing to its close;
  The shadows lengthen down the hill;
  The sounds of joy are growing still;
The western sky wears tints of rose.

I drink the beauties of the scene,
  While mingling thoughts of joy and woe—
  Oh! who can all the secret know
Of restless heart and quiet mien?

The world may count me as content;
   Deceit I see, and give deceit;
   Yet wish for one true heart to greet
With trust for trust, forever blent.

Oh! is the world so wrapt in sin
   That all pure confidence and trust
   Lies lost and hidden in the dust
That fell from years that once have been?

I rise, as night comes creeping on,
   And ramble down the hillside slope;
   In realms of shadow is my hope;
I cherish most that which is gone.

### III.

So disconnected runs my theme
   That those who read may, smiling, say:
   " 'Tis all a waste—time mused away
In idling through a gloomy dream."

But hours like this may cheer the heart,
   And soothe the mind, though trouble-tossed,
   While dwelling on some blessing lost
That once has been of life a part.

A quiet time, in which we view
   The world that seems all peace and joy;
   Then calmly scan the base alloy
That intermixes with the true.

So, as the dark is closing in,
   In from the world I go to rest,
   And deem my life, though little blest,
At least removed from crime and sin.

# PART SECOND.

---

---

## TOO LATE.

Just here, beside the stile,
We will stop and rest awhile.
And we'll talk of the times that are o'er, Ned.
I like to watch your face,
Though it lacks the boyish grace
That made it once so bright and fair, Ned.

You say you've come to see
If there is a change in me—
In my heart as well as in my face, Ned.
Well, don't say that I forget,
Or call me cold and set,
When I say that all is past—all past, Ned.

In the early morn of life,
I'd fain have been your wife;
But not now—it is over now, Ned;
Too long we've walked apart,
The summer of the heart
Blooms but once for every life, Ned.

The friends we loved are dead,
And with their presence fled
The flower and freshness of our lives, Ned;
The noon of life is past,
And the time is coming fast
When the world will know us nevermore, Ned.

Though the mem'ry of the spring
Will make the wild bird sing
'Midst the gloom of winter days, Ned;
The words of love you speak,
But make the gloom more bleak,
In the winter of my lonely heart, Ned.

They can but give me pain,
For my heart has dormant lain
These many long and weary years, Ned;
And nothing change can make,
Though I've suffered for your sake,
And you once were all the world to me, Ned.

I can grant no boon you crave,
For only in the grave
I look for quiet from the world, Ned.
Perhaps it is but right,
That our lives have proved a blight,
And I ask not who's to blame, you or I, Ned?


## THE COTTAGE BY THE GREAT HOUSE.

The light from a crimson sunset
    Gleams o'er his lordship's lands,
O'er gardens, fair and blooming,
    Near where the great house stands.

I look on the shining window,
  Where madam sits and dreams,
While the rich, old velvet curtains,
  Grow bright in the day-god's beams.

Ah! madam is rich and haughty,
  The lord is proud and cold,
But they dote on their son so handsome,
  Brave Cleon, fair and bold.

The world has said that Cleon
  Cares not for gold or fame,
He loves his dogs and hunting-horn,
  The cup and the social game.

They say he has no heart for love,
  No praise for beauty's shrine,
That the only pleasures of his life
  Are the chase and the sparkling wine.

But little do they know of him,
  Who prate this o'er and o'er,
I read his secret long ago,
  As I sat at my cottage door.

He loves a lady, fair and good,
  Across the feathery tide,
And the greatest pleasure of his life
  He finds when by her side.

Though many maids may sigh and rave
  About his golden hair,
And say it is a shame to have
  No heart with form so fair.

But little he will reck that they
  Are dying for a glance,
As at the banquet or the rout
  He joins in play or dance.

So still we ponder, day by day,
    This secret o'er and o'er,
*He* at the great house window,
    And *I* at the cottage door.


### UNSATISFIED.

Across the weary lapse of years,
That made my heart so strangely cold,
O'er days that lie 'twixt then and now,
Through which I've borne a grief untold,
Last night, while earth was wrapped in sleep,
And all was still upon the sea—
Sweet Fancy wove a dream and brought
My girlhood's idol back to me.

I felt his touch upon my curls—
I felt his kind eyes read my face;
I looked once more upon that form—
So perfect in its manly grace.
He told me how his soul had been
So true to me, and then he smiled
And said that he had come to claim
The heart I gave him when a child.

He stooped and took me in his arms,
And pressed upon my lips the kiss
That I had hungered for, for years,
And asked of fate no boon but this—
To live again that vanished hour,
To hear him say his love was mine,
To feel that kiss upon my lips,
To have his arms around me twine,
To look into his tender eyes,
And hear his words so fond and low,

I'd barter all the rest of life,
It's poorer triumphs *all* forego.

O God! let those whose youth has gone,
Wasted in sordid strife for gain,
Whose hearts have never quickened yet,
But to some selfish hope attain;
Whose spirits scarcely soar above
The leaden clods they plow and till,
Scorn love like this—I but despise
Each grinning, mawkish imbecile.
The thoughts that glow with endless life,
The voice whose music charms away,
All taint of earthly care, is *still*
And *cold*, to eyes and ears of *clay*.
But since we've faith that all is well,
Subservient to a ruling power,
Their *being*, then, is not in vain;
So, let them live their little hour,
Within a narrow, cheerless round,
Monotonous, with selfish strife,
To stir their sluggish blood enough
To keep ablaze the lamp of life;
Perchance in realms of love and light
Their feeble spirits will expand,
Their dark and meager souls at last
Illumined in another land.

The morning sunlight kissed the hills—
I woke from sleep in trembling tears—
Woke from the dream that gave to me
More joy than I had known for years.
The world looks very fair to-day—
Our hills are sweet with flowers of spring;
White clouds are drifting o'er the sky,
And in the trees the wild birds sing.

But in my soul there is a gloom
That I had thought was passed away,
And it will shadow all my life,
Till breaks the great Eternal Day.
The love that, if not dead, I hoped
Had found a long and lasting sleep,
Still burns within my spirit's depths—
I kneel before its shrine and weep.

My soul has known but one ideal—
But one sweet mem'ry fills my heart—
I have not seen his face for years,
And we are drifting far apart.
And though my life seems strangely blest,
My early dream grows dearer yet—
While life and thought are still my own,
My idol I can not forget.


OROVILLE, 1868.

The clouds of poverty are all about me,
My young heart sad, my sky without one ray,
But I know that God looks on me in the darkness,
And he sees and listens while I work and pray.

The way is strange, my life's path steep and rugged,
And envious foes are near me to defame,
But the mighty hand of God can guide me upward,
And on the scroll of worth inscribe my name.

No human power can long prevail against me,
Nor change the upward tendence of my way,
For that All-seeing Eye has sought and found me,
And safe from wrong is leading me to-day.

God bless the few true ones who are around me,
And bless each thoughtless and unfeeling churl;
I pity all who blame, and in their blindness
Would deem so weak a poor and friendless girl.

In hearts far, far above their own so craven,
My acts shall build a long-enduring shrine
Where age and youth shall bring alike their blessings,
And lay them there, to be forever mine.


## THE DYING GAMBLER.

Come here, beside me, Nellie,
    That fearful delirium is past,
There are things I'd like to say,
    The words that I know will be my last.

For, Nellie, I am dying,
    All the work of the demons is done,
I've bartered my life for vice,
    And its rule, and my own race, is run.

I want to tell you, Nellie,
    That I'm sorry for all that has been,
And the thought is hard to bear,
    That I've broken *your heart* with my sin.

For, Nellie, I *have loved you*,
    In spite of my love for cards and wine,
And I always saw your eyes
    Watching from out its devilish shine.

You've been a good wife, Nellie,
    Too good for a thankless wretch like me.
Raise up my head a little,
    There—my breath does not come very free.

You remember, I promised
To cherish you all the rest of life,
On that morn so long ago,
When we were first called man and wife.

How bright the future looked,
Full of good resolves; I meant them all.
It seems the worst of curses,
On a drunken wretch, like me, should fall.

But you are weeping, Nellie,
For a miserable brute, like me?
Stoop down once more and kiss me,
It grows dark soon, I can scarcely see.

And you have loved me well,
You do yet, in face of wrong and shame:
Nellie, if I get better,
I will try to deserve it again.

But no, it's no use, Nellie;
But I do repent of all my sin;
Pray—I'm your husband, Nellie,
It's no matter what else I have been.

Pray that my soul be ransomed,
When I'm put away under the sod;
You said once that 'twas written,
No drunkards enter the kingdom of God.

Well, I've gambled, and drank too,
With the worst; and many sprees I've seen,
But 'twas playing the "deuce" though,
All the time, and misusing my "queen."

And you, the prettiest card,
By far, Nellie, that I ever struck,
I never half deserved you,
But "helped my hand" in a run o' luck.

There are many more, Nellie,
　Making a " flowery play " and high,
But the risk won't seem too great,
　Till at last, like me, they come to die,

They'll always hang to the cards,
　Till at last they draw the " ace of spades,"
And find the game "played out,"
　As every hope of "a winning " fades.

You've seen the worst of the game,
　Your "draw " was nothing but tears and woe,
But you hold the "pat hand " now
　Of the two, were you "called " to go.

Mine's a poor one to ''show down,"
　And if I could, I would "pass " or "bluff,"
But that wouldn't win anyhow,
　I "went blind," so I " stand," but it's rough.

You have half your chances left,
　I can't "back in," for I've "gone clean through."
O God! must I leave the game?
　Life a " dead loss" to myself *and you.*

There's nothing hurts a loser
　Like to sum up, *too late,* all his loss;
I threw a man's best chance away,
　For industry and honesty's " boss."

Life's been a " misdeal," Nellie;
　But may be, though dark the way I've trod,
A soul as lost as my own,
　At the last can make its peace with God.

## IN MY ALBUM.

When I look on those two faces,
While remembrance sweetly traces,
O'er the features fair and perfect,
    Each expression they have worn;
When I note the proud lips molded
Like a rose leaf, curved and folded,
Comes a dream divine, untarnished
    By the world's cold pride and scorn.

When I watch the dreamy languor,
And the deep and soulful splendor
Of the eyes, that, dark-impassioned,
    Still are frank and true and pure,
All my soul grows fond and fonder,
As I sit and muse and wonder
When will come that day of rapture,
    That will all their joy insure.

Well I know the wealth of feeling
Those bright faces are revealing,
And I read the guarded secret,
    *Why* they lie there, side by side;
Yes, I read the old, old story:
In the strength of life's young glory,
*He* is all her hope and sunlight,
    And *she* is his promised bride.

Oh! I pray no gloom of sorrow,
Waiting in some far to-morrow,
May come o'er those lives so faithful,
    All their peace and trust to blast;
For I know on this dream's ending,
All their happiness is pending,
And upon one turn of fortune,
    All their destiny is cast.

Rather than distrust should ever
Wide and cruelly dissever
Those two beings, always kindred
   In each thought and word and look,
Better death should o'er them hover,
And their forms now darkly cover—
Take them to the life eternal,
   Face to face, as in this book.

## ISABEL.

If all the sheep in the fold were white—
If all the days in the year were fair—
If never a note of sadness woke
From boughs that sway in the summer air—

If the paths where wander tiny feet
Were never filled with thorns and snares—
If all the flowers in the field were fresh,
And never bloomed among the tares—

If all in the world was pure and good—
If life was forever free from pain—
If the heart could know no weariness,
I would wish my darling back again.

But o'er the threshold of time and care,
Her fair young soul has safely crossed,
And never in this world will she grieve
O'er a blighted hope or a purpose lost.

And in the scenes of the after-land,
Where streams of silvery brightness flow,
Where flowers are sweet in lasting bloom,
Where the weary soul oft longs to go—

She wanders, blessed for evermore,
With a spirit bright and pure and free,
And I do not wish her back again,
For I know she waits to welcome me.


## MY IDEAL.

When and how shall I meet my darling?
What are the things our hearts will say?
How will the years that perhaps dissever
Our kindred beings be swept away?

Perhaps, o'er the hills of our golden country,
Wanders the spirit that waits for me—
Perchance, till I cross the dim, dark valley,
My Ideal's face I ne'er shall see!

Whether his hair is black or golden,
Whether his eyes are dark or blue,
I care not, so that his soul be perfect,
To pride and honor leal and true.

When and how shall I meet my darling?
What are the words which our troth will seal?
Where, in this world of sin and sorrow,
Will I meet and welcome—my soul's Ideal?


## JUNE.

O June, fair June! O month of bloom!
When on the air so slumb'rously
Floats subtile perfumes rare and sweet,
Red roses glow upon thy breast,
And berries gleam beneath thy feet.

O month of songs! to thee belongs
The best of earth's intensity;
Thy fields are bright with yellow wheat,
That finds new beauty 'neath thy smile,
And shimmers in thy golden heat.

O month of dreams! there ever seems
A tint of splendor in thy air;
Oh! bring to me again those hours
When summer reigned, and my sad heart
Was blest, within thy fragrant bowers.

O month of rest! thy hours so blest
Brought to my life its lasting crown;
I love thy sunset's red'ning glow,
Thy birds and flowers, that bring to me
The dream I dreamed one year ago.

O month of bloom! when in the tomb
The sun of life sinks down for me,
Then let my cold, still face be hid
By sweet June roses, rich and rare,
Strewn 'neath my somber coffin's lid.


## ELMER KELLER.

I dream of gentle winds that play,
    And flowers that to their wanderings wave,
Upon the hillside slope to-day
    Around my little Elmer's grave.

The wild dove's plaintive note will come,
    And o'er his rest will hum the bee;
Each season brings its changing charms—
    But *he* will never come to me.

Oh! let the gentle tear-drop flow—
　　Though sad, my grief to me is sweet,
For paths of sin will never know
　　The wanderings of his little feet.

He knows a fairer world than this,
　　And fairer flowers that never die—
He once has known a mother's kiss—
　　He ne'er will know a mother's sigh.

But still I cannot help but weep—
　　The weakness of all earth is mine,
I long for little arms in sleep
　　That round my neck were wont to twine.

But oh! I know, some future day,
　　When I am laid beneath the sod,
I'll find my darling far away
　　Among the blooming fields of God.


## TUBEROSES.

### DUNHAM FARM, MARCH 10, 1868.

They put them into the hands of the dead,
They wreathe them about the face,
When the soul has fled beyond returning,
And the loving heart has lost its yearning,
Beneath death's chilling trace.

I have gathered these—O darling!—darling—
Let not your eyes reproachful seem to be,
Pity the heart that in unspoken anguish,
Far from their light, for evermore must languish—
*You* must be as dead to *me*.

Into your strong hands, from mine, weak, trembling
I put them. Round your worshiped face,
In my fond fancy I will see them lying,
While pure, within me, is my spirit dying,
I will shun my heart's disgrace.

Oh! forget not—when you see them blooming,
Think they spring above my grave,
Where wild temptation can assail no longer,
I go, while yet my soul is stronger,
And the grace of God can save.

## SONG.

When I am with thee, the cold world forgetting,
Happy, contented, I live but for thee;
But when we are parted, I'm half broken-hearted,
And weary and sad are the hours that I see.

Oft when I meet thee in scenes of pleasure,
With those that love thee gathering near,
If, 'mid joys beguiling, I see thee smiling,
My foolish heart trembles with unspoken fear.

If they should take thee from me forever,
No other could waken the love of my heart;
No bright eyes in glancing, by sweetly entrancing,
Could make me forget that we were apart.

My thoughts would still linger around thee forever,
Though smiles might allure, and flattery delude,
No ceasing of sorrow, by time could I borrow,
Since thy smiles had won me, and thy voice had sued.

3

## TO MOTHER, WHEN LITTLE ELMORE DIED.

Parted by death—are we parted forever?
Till we meet on the shore of the beautiful river,
Baby has gone in his innocent beauty;
I weep; while they tell me submission is duty.

If he had lived through the years of his childhood,
Reaching the pride of a beautiful manhood,
The hour would have come when we must dissever,
May be for long years, and may be forever.

Then better it is that in death he is sleeping,
Though it leaves me the pain, the grief, and the weeping,
Than to have him away, in forbidden paths straying,
My heart worn by suspense, and his by delaying.

He never will stand at that threshold of sorrow—
The place where a mother shakes hands with her dar-
  ling—
And say, when I ask, "how long must we sever?"
"May be for years, mother; may be forever."

No, he is safe from trouble and danger,
Unconscious of crime—to sinning a stranger;
I can sit by his grave and say, 'midst my weeping,
"God make me worthy of Baby's next greeting."

Though parted by death, not parted forever,
We will meet on the shore of the beautiful river;
This world is the portal we pass to another,
And my Baby'll be first to welcome his mother.

## AT LAST.

When the last sad sigh is o'er,
    When the heart is stilled forever,
When the spirit seeks the shore,
    Leading down to death's dark river;

O'er eternity's great wave,
    *Then* at last is found fruition;
For each hope we fondly crave,
    For the wildest heart's petition.

Broken then the barriers down,
    Here that kindred lives dissever,
Fate's decree or fortune's frown
    Comes to part or pain us never.

Midst the rose and lilies bloom,
    On the isles of sweet contentment,
Lost the darkness of the tomb,
    Lost the pang of fierce resentment.

Envy with malignant hand
    Ne'er shall wake a tone discordant,
Spirits in that after-land
    Beam with loveliness transcendent.

Love, not hate, will reign supreme,
    Free from dross and earth's pollution,
Then we realize the dream
    Springing from the soul's ambition.

When the book of life is closed,
    Clasped by death's remorseless fingers,
O'er the records there reposed
    Then the eye of justice lingers.

And what proves our trials here,
 Is by mercy's hand arighted,
No temptations then allure,
 Then no cherished hope is blighted.

When the last sad sigh is o'er,
 When life's day has closed forever,
Pure and free for evermore,
 Sin shall part and pain us never.


## TIRED.

Out upon life's ocean sailing
 In my frail life barque,
I have watched the storm-clouds gather
 Till my sky is dark.

Though the waves for some are smiling,
 I hear but their roar,
While the rest are onward steering,
 I would drop the oar.

I could shun the rocks of danger,
 And the breakers brave,
Till the only heart that loved me
 Sank beneath the wave.

I heed not the craft around me;
 In the distant west
Lie the isles where I am going,
 To the port of rest.

But I can not wait the voyage
 That will take me o'er;
Like the sea-bird, in the twilight,
 I will seek the shore.

Like the swallows southward flying
   From a stormy clime,
I, when warned of coming danger,
   Take my flight in time.     ·

For the storms I can not weather,
   In my fair, frail boat,
Sin's dark waters will o'ercome me,
   If I onward float.

And I fear, on hidden shallows,
   That my barque will strand;
Where the bars of dread temptation
   Wash their glittering sand.

So, while still the fleet is sailing
   To the far-off shore,
I, while rocked in troubled waters,
   Drop my silent oar.

## SONG.

I have spoken the words that must sever,
   I have sundered every tie;
The charms of our lost love never
   Will gladden you and I.

I have sealed the vow that has parted,
   And I stoop to wear the chain,
That is making me broken-hearted,
   Since we never must meet again.

The years are like midnight seeming,
   That lie 'twixt me and the grave;
We have been so long at our dreaming,
   That nothing our peace can save.

I have spoken the words that must sever,
I have sundered every tie,
The charms of our lost love never
Will gladden you and I.

## AFTER THE STORM.

Over the world the clouds wept to-day,
But the wind and the rain are passing away;
Gone is the gloom that drooped like a pall,
And the wealth of God's sunshine is over it all.

I think of the clouds that far in the past,
The beautiful day of my childhood o'ercast,
Of the tears that in sorrow and silence I shed,
When the blossoms of hope seemed faded and dead.

And I feel in my heart, how much this bright hour,
Where the splendor of sunshine follows the shower,
Resembles the life, once gloomy and sad,
But at last, like to-day, is resplendent and glad.

Then let the clouds weep, the storms sigh and rave,
The rains dress the turf o'er the loneliest grave;
Although clouds of sorrow droop like a pall,
The light of God's mercy is over us all.

## TO M. M. S.

O Mattie! come back from the shadowy shore,
And lay your fair hand on my head,
And tell me, my darling, I only have dreamed
That they number your name with the dead.

Ah! when the soft sunshine of spring comes once more,
  And the flowers wave and smile in the breeze,
When the fields are so fresh, and the world looks so bright,
  And the birds sing so sweet through the trees,

One life will be cheerless, no sunshine can come
  To my soul, from the landscape or wave;
For they've laid you away from my sight, and my heart
  Has gone down, with its pride, to the grave.

No more can I hear the soft tone of your voice,
  Or watch the blush ebb from your cheek,
As your fringed eyelids drooped, with a shy, modest grace,
  O'er those blue orbs, so tenderly meek.

For now the true heart that was mine—only mine,
  Lies still in the hush of the tomb,
And the delicate hands are folded so close,
  And your lips have grown cold in its gloom.

O Mattie! I pray, from the dim afterland,
  That your spirit may smile upon me,
And guide me aright till I sit at your feet,
  From this pain and this sorrowing free.


### VALLEYREST.

I love the little valley, amid the Wyandotte hills;
  When I found the sweet retreat, May was blooming o'er
    its green,
And no friends so dear to me as those who loved me there,
  Though the bridal, and the tomb, and the years, have
    come between.

And that stream of crystal water, where the broad, green
    rushes grow,
How many a summer noontide, beside its restless sheen,
I laughed, beneath the drooping oaks, the summer hours
    away,
    With Emmaline and Sallie, or Cal and Josephine.

But time has made sad changes, as it touched each sepa-
    rate heart,
And many a day of sorrow since then we *all* have seen,
And *one* has proved a traitor to the friendship fond of old,
    And as dead to me and mine is poor, faithless Josephine.

Still, looking back to-day, I see a picture fair,
    The valley and the streamlet, the flowers, and birds,
    and bees;
A happy lot we were, within the quiet bounds
    Of the hillsides rising upward, from beyond the grand
    old trees.

But as I dream of Valleyrest, one winsome face I see,
    With a white brow framed in beauty, by a wealth of
    rippling hair,
The rose of youth and health aglow, upon the rounded
    cheek,
    And lips that seemed to have always, but tender smiles
    to wear.

And of all the things I loved, among the Wyandotte hills,
    The truest was *your heart*, through a hyacinthine shine,
It looked from out your eyes, unchanged—unchanging still,
    As mine will ever beat for you, my darling Emmaline.

So I love the little valley that nestles in the hills;
    'Twas a place of rest to me, and its spell will not depart,
Nor the memory of that summer I lived there long ago,
    When I learned the first sweet lessons that woke my
    girlish heart.

## AFTER DEATH.

Sweet flowers strew over my quiet heart,
Scatter them round my bier, .
I, who have loved them so well in life,
In death would have them near.

By a window low, in a western room,
Lay me at day's decline,
And lift the lace from the glistening pane,
Just where the last rays shine.

And let the blessed sunlight fall
Aslant my poor, pale face,
Where nevermore the hand of Time
The lines of care will trace.

The late sunshine among the flowers
I've loved since childhood's days,
And through the fields at sunset ran
Amid the golden haze.

And when the eyes, that loved the light so well.
Grown dim, have looked their last,
And turned their gaze beyond this world,
And closed on all the past,

I'd have the sunshine and the rose
Blend o'er my pulseless breast.
Where day's last beam smiles o'er my grave,
Oh! leave me to my rest.


### FRAGMENT.

Like the bird, with tender song,
Singing all the long day through,
So art thou, O heart of mine!
But a trembling minstrel, too.

And as birdie sings farewell
To the nest that was her home,
Plumes her wings to cross the wave,
In an unknown clime to roam;

So my soul some day will pour
All its wealth in grieving songs,
As it takes uncertain flight
To the realm where it belongs.


## IN MEMORY OF L. L. W.

### TO LIZZIE.

The sunlight gleams across the palings white and still,
On the tombstones and the graves, out upon the slanting
     hill,
Where, through the lonesome day, my darling and my hope
Lies so quietly asleep, on the hillside's sunny slope.

I sit and watch the graves, and dream of days gone by,
Till my heart grows cold and sad, and I wish that I could
     die,
Exchanging all the world—its wealth, its joy, and pride—
For a sweet and quiet slumber near to my darling's side.

They come and speak kind words, and tell me I'll forget
That life is long, and still must hold much gladness for me
     yet.
Oh! could they see his presence is the only thing I crave,
They'd leave me, knowing all my hope was buried in his
     grave.

So long, day after day, I wait and dream apart,
While our baby's life is throbbing, beneath my throbbing
     heart,
I weep, and fondly pray that I may sometime trace
The features of its father in its little angel face.

But I feel within my soul that the palings white and still,
And the little mound of earth out upon the slanting hill,
Hold all the best this world and life's young promise gave,
And I know my heart is buried within my husband's grave.

## INTEMPERANCE.

There walks a fiend o'er our beautiful earth,
His wiles are crafty and strong,
Wherever he stalks in his terrible might
He hushes the sweet voice of song.

He quenches the smile of the trusting young bride;
He brings the poor mother's despair;
He blights the fair lives of the good and the true,
With the weight of wearisome care.

He withers the flowers of friendship and love
With the breath of his poisonous flame;
He robs the pure young of their promising hopes,
And the good of a virtuous name.

Incarnate this demon of woe and of want,
He comes with a soft, subtle tread,
And leads the unwary adown to the gloom
That shadows the poor drunkard's head.

*His* task is to lurk in the glittering bowl,
And smile from the red, sparkling wine;
To hate and defy him with tongue and with pen,
And thwart him through life, will be *mine.*

The young, tender hand of an innocent child
Once saved a great city of old,
And the flood that crept on to o'erwhelm and destroy,
By that brave touch was stayed and controlled.

So the frail hand of woman, if clutched on the throat
Of this demon, will crush out his breath,
And take from the face of our beautiful earth
This foul emissary of death.


## SONOMA.

A picture lives within my memory,
Of one sweet smile upon our State's fair face,
That shone upon my heart awhile, and left
Forever there the impress of its grace.

A glimpse of generous autumn's quiet fields,
Whose broad expanse then bore the harvest-track,
Through which the cruel blade had found its way,
And marked its traces with the golden stack.

And vineyards laden, while the setting sun
Distilled the wine, within their purple wealth,
And peaceful homes, where sheltered kindly hearts,
And children rosy with the glow of health.


## FRAGMENT.

'Tis well that you lie in your lonely grave,
Where the stars of the winter night look down
On the varied scenes of the distant town;
But my heart goes back, and pauses there,
In the tender hush of muttered prayer,
As I dream of the words that you used to crave.

The sullen waves of the ebbing years
Have borne me back to a seeming rest;
But some of the things that were blest and best
Lie in the distance; and songs will die
On my lips, sometimes, when joy seems nigh,
And I turn away in blinding tears.

## THE DYING BOY.

My little hands are weary,
My heart beats strangely slow,
And my mamma is crying,
While they whisper: " He must go."

The fever, it has left me
So thin, so pale, and weak,
I think I'll never move again,
And I do not care to speak.

I am going o'er the river,
Where, I've heard my aunty say,
All the little children gather
In a bright, eternal day;

Where flowers are always blooming
In a radiance rare and sweet;
Where no paths of sin are waiting
The tread of little feet.

I wish papa could show me
The way to find that shore;
But oh! he can't go with me,
For he can not leave his store.

He must stay, and get some dollars,
He's not an hour to lose;
He don't get time to go to church,
Or even read the news;

He works all day, and Sunday, too,
He has to buy nice clothes
For sister Madge—my big sister—
She has so many beaux,

And goes out to the theater,
And to parties, every night;
And once she left me all alone
In my room, without a light.

I wasn't much afraid, but cried,
Not from the fear of harm;
But she never stayed one evening
With me since I was born.

And mamma has so much to do,
With company all day;
And nurse is always cross and mean,
Because I'm in the way.

I don't know why they make a fuss,
Look sorry so, and cry;
Nobody'll have to tend to me,
And scold me, if I die.

I never seemed o' much account,
And always broke my toys—
There did n't seem no place, at all,
A' purpose for little boys.

So I will try and not be 'fraid,
And let my papa stay;
And maybe God will send some one
To meet me on the way.

He sent me to this awful place,
So full of tears and pain;
And surely, if I want to go,
He'll take me home again.

## FRAGMENT.

In the days that have flown
We have drifted apart,
And my voice o'er the waves,
Can not reach to your heart;
Unbroken the silence that came with the years,
And the spell undissolved by the magic of tears.

## TO AMY.

May thy blue eyes never dim with sorrow;
May thy young heart beat for ever free from care;
And the years, for thee, my little sister,
Their brightest smiles and blessings ever wear.

May thy joyous feet go safely onward
Through the morning flowers that strew thy happy way,
While the promise fair that greets thy spring-time,
But ushers in the glad and perfect day.

In its golden heat, oh! never falter;
Let thy soul, above its splendor, ever soar
To a future where the flowers fade not,
And daytime ends in darkness nevermore.

## "REMEMBER ME."

A little band of purest gold,
That bears those two words, sad, yet sweet,
Gleams on my hand; I watch its sheen,
And ask when we again shall meet.

Remem'bring you, what do I see?
A boyish face, and curling hair,
Brown eyes that greet with truth my own,
A forehead white, and broad, and fair.

Remember—oh! could I forget
Those days of bright and transient bloom ?
Not till my requiem be sung,
And mourners bear me to the tomb.

Those days—my heart grows faint and cold,
As over them I think and weep;
Ah! then my life was blest with hopes
That now, alas! forever sleep.

And memory does beside recall
So much that I would fain forget—
So much of misery and pain—
Such dreams of stars forever set.

My life has been so full of care,
And never from its burden free,
My heart is old before its time—
I've left you far away from me.

And though the morning of our lives
Dawned almost on the self-same day,
*I've* lived long years *you* have not known,
And left you, oh! so far away.

Yes, far away, in youth's proud hope,
*So far* from what my life must be;
I often wonder why you find
A friend congenial in me.

You tell me that my eyes are bright,
That roses bloom upon my cheek—
I would that you could read to-day
The story I will never speak.

A record traced in cruel lines
By destiny, and never told;
Then would you know all I have borne,
And *why* my heart has grown so old.

I would not say these plaintive things,
Dear friend of mine; but then, you see
My heart is moved—this tiny gift
Bears on its face: " Remember me."


## MENDOCINO.

A willing, fair, and perfect child,
In joyous eagerness to-day she stands
To meet her mother's smile, and bear
The fruitful training of her gentle hands.

Her redwood groves, they sing a living song;
Her rivers to the sea rich greeting bear;
Her farms are nestled in the vales,
Her hills a smiling prospect wear.

Within her bounds dwell sons of noble toil,
Whose lives in usefulness seem half divine,
Within their hearts the echoed truth
Of words thus offered at their county's shrine.

There is no place for apes of fashion here;
No painted dolls, or votaries of pride;
An honest name and undefiled,
This do they prize more than the world beside.

God bless the earnest, peaceful hearts that know
The quiet joys that fill the farmer's life;
And bless the ones who share their lot,
The careful mother, and the faithful wife.

4

## LIFE.

What's life? To live is but to love,
Then see the loved upon the bier,
And drop the mourner's bitter tear.

Thus, as we strive to fill with ease
The last days of a mother's life,
She falters—droops amid the strife.

Her dear form fills the winding-sheet
Beneath the dark and somber pall
That folds in gloom our hope—our all.

We stand beside the yawning grave,
While clods sound on the coffin-lid
'Neath which our precious dead lies hid.

Our hearts are dumb with silent woe;
The star that led our steps aright
Hath set in mystery's awful night.

As years roll on, some spark of hope
Burns in the once despairing breast—
Again we dream of earthly rest.

Some one is left to love and guide—
A brother or a sister dear
Still dries the sad, desponding tear.

When, lo! the angel's wing is spread,
White hands are folded o'er the breast
That has, for aye, found peace and rest.

The light that burned in soul-lit eyes
Is darkly quenched forevermore,
No years can e'er the loss restore.

We take one lock of silken hair,
Press down the eyelids still and cold,
And lay the form beneath the mold.

Once more the gloom has chilled the soul—
A longer time is wrapt in woe
The heart, as seasons come and go.

Again we love, and court the spell;
The glances of some tender eye
Have bound once more the silken tie.

A love by which all else seems cold
We find, to bless us on our way;
In paths of bliss our footsteps stray.

But as we wander, hand in hand,
Adown life's autumn-day hillside,
Why do we start and turn aside?

There sits "the shadow feared by man;"
Shedding a still more blighting frost—
At last all earthly hope is lost.

For, sundered is the last dear tie—
No more we seek, no more we find
A sympathy among our kind.

Still down the hill of life we go,
Around whose base dark shadows crowd,
While falls a roaring deep and loud,

Where breakers in their thunder hoarse
Wake music thrillingly sublime
Upon the rugged shores of Time.

At last we find that sunset's glow
Has brought to us the phantom bark
Which bears us o'er the waters dark.

As life has been a troubled dream,
We meet the change with wearied soul,
And gladly seek the promised goal.

Earth knows us once, but will no more—
Perchance the islands of the blest
Will yield to us a port of rest.

At least, we know a gracious God
Will guard us with a watchful eye,
Though only mystery we descry.

That Power, which marks the sparrow's fall,
Will make disposal of each soul
That soars beyond this world's control.


### DEAD.

All day the grasses move and play
    Upon the slanting, flowery hill,
While wild doves mourn, and brown bees hum,
And larks with joyous warbling come
    Where I am lying still.

They say that I'm at rest at last,
    As mute, enchained by death, I lie,
And hear them talk of rest profound,
Found only 'neath some solemn mound,
    With face turned to the sky.

Thus, day by day, they come, they go,
    While winds first murmur, sob, then sigh;
The grass grows yellow on the hill,
But yet I'm lying cold and still,
    While seasons bloom and die.

Sometimes upon the lettered stone
    That stands above my fallen head
A lonely songster sits and sings;
It brings a dream of vanished springs,
    And I forget I'm dead.

One day *he* came—his well-known step
 In any clime or world I'd know;
And death is not a dreamless sleep,
'Tis oft oblivious, but not deep,
 Though all may deem it so.

I knew the old, familiar touch,
 He stroked the grass above my breast;
I thrilled beneath the coffin lid—
Thank God! the secret lay well hid,
 He thought I was at rest.

I love the flowers and sunshine well,
 I love the voice of singing bird—
But oh! I loved *his presence* more;
I'd never longed to move before,
 Or make my feelings heard.

He laid his head upon my grave,
 He wept as *man alone* can weep,
The tears came o'er his dark blue eyes,
Like rain aslant fair summer skies—
 He said: "Why must you sleep?"

What agony to be so near,
 And yet so far—so far apart,
To hear him weeping 'midst the flowers,
Those fair, brown curls I've toyed for hours,
 Above my pulseless heart.

O God! how much I craved the power
 To lay my hand upon his head,
E'en to forego all heavenly bliss,
For just one more caress or kiss;
 But then you know I'm dead.

No touch of cheek, or hand, or lip,
  Is left in life for us to know;
For, though our love was true and fond,
My being drifted far beyond—
  *But oh! I loved him so.*

How lone I felt when he had gone;
  And, listening to his rapid tread
Go echoing faint and fainter down
The narrow path that leads to town,
  Recalled the words he said:

" Why must you sleep ? "  I do not sleep,
  Although my heart is turned to dust,
Some spell has fallen o'er my eyes,
Which breaks when all the dead arise;
  Till *then*, be dumb, I must.

So let the grasses creep above
  My prison walls so desolate;
It must be right—so let it be;
I wait—in future I may see
  The higher aim of fate.


### STRANDED.

I stand upon the rugged shore
That bounds the western sea;
The restless waves, on wings of foam,
Bear kisses to the lea.

The March winds sweep the grasses green,
That tremble 'neath my feet;
The few wild flowers, just newly born,
Look up with faces sweet.

By voices sad of wind and wave,
In duets strange and wild,
And bars of thrilling melody,
My fancy is beguiled.

Beneath the wild and barren cliff,
Where breakers moan and roar,
A bark amidst the cruel rocks
Lies moored for evermore.

Like some lone bird with weary wing
She flew before the storm;
And, rocked upon the ruthless waves,
Seemed trembling with alarm.

In sunny splendor of to-day
I find no shade of gloom
That wrapt the ocean as a pall,
And brought her to her doom.

But though the sky is blue—serene,
And winds blow soft and free,
Her sails will ne'er unfurl again,
To sweep the restless sea.

By isles of bloom and pleasant lands,
Where smiles a sunny shore;
Where spice winds kiss the orange groves,
In pride she'll sail no more.

Upon the sullen sea of life,
Float many barks to-day;
We launch them with a precious freight,
And watch them drift away.

Some, borne by breezes swift and strong
To isles so fair and bright,
Find harbor and again return
With speed and wings of light.

While others, full of hope and love,
Fade from our anxious gaze;
We pace with aching heart the shore
Through long and weary days.

We look where waves and waters meet,
Longing to greet the sail,
'Till the heart is sick with yearning,
And the lips grow cold and pale;

Then, as we stand in silent woe,
With anxious, outstretched hands,
Brought by the waves that touch our feet,
A waif lies on the sands.

We stoop—and lo! 'tis a relic—
All that is left to tell
Of the fated ship now stranded,
That we had loved so well.

There are barks that sailed away
In the dim and distant years,
Fraught with treasures of heart and soul,
Laden with hopes and fears.

We pace the shore, and listen long
In wild unease and pain;
We mourn and weep our lives away,
They never return again.

O Power! that bids the wave be still,
Pity each breaking heart
That has trusted and lost its all
On some ship that it saw depart;

And teach us, as they drift away,
Sailing early or late,
We will find them safely moored inside
The *beautiful Golden Gate*.

# PART THIRD.

## HUMBOLDT.

The mem'ry of thy sunny vales
  Sleeps in my heart;
Where berries gleamed in golden heat
Beneath June's softly ling'ring feet;
Where, on the summer's slumb'rous breast,
The winds the yielding days caressed.

Thy blossoms, wet with fragrant dew,
  Have brushed my cheek;
While wandering in thy woods along,
I heard the birds' exquisite song,
And marveled not that life should seem
So like a sweet, delicious dream.

From streams of water cold and pure,
  My lips have quaffed;
Where, in thy forests dark and deep,
The somber shadows seem to sleep;
Where pallid lilies bloom and die,
Denied the radiance of the sky.

My wand'ring feet went o'er thy hills
   In sweet content;
That destiny to me assigned
A pleasant task of heart and mind;
And led me, for a little while,
Beneath the blessing of thy smile.

The glorious promise of thy years
   Spoke to my soul;
And in the future thou shalt meet
A grand fruition, proud and sweet;
And bloom, untouched by blight or ban,
A country blessed by God and man.

## LINES.

In the halls of recollection—on their magic stair,
I have paused with look uplifted
To a picture there.
Tenderly, from out the framing of the vanished past,
Smiles a face whose eyes upon me
Long have looked their last.

Eyes that gave in sweetest off'ring all that lips could say
Of a love that lives; though living,
Now has passed away;
For that heart that once so fondly beat with hope and truth,
While its crimson tide was glowing
With the warmth of youth.

And I pause within the quiet that we only reach
When the years have brought a sorrow
Too intense for speech.
When the soul bows down in anguish at some altar-stone,
Whence the worshipers have vanished,
Till we kneel *alone*.

When the world's cold rays have chilled us,
And the tears that start
In an anguished pride are banished
Backward to the heart,
There to fall in bitter weeping, drop by drop, and day by
    day,
Till its happy songs are silenced,
And its gladness worn away.

Here I lift my hands up meekly, and I kneel and pray,
Here within the mystic splendor, shining from that distant
    day,
That this sad—this last petition,
May yet meet thy tender grace,
While those eyes give out their blessing
On my upturned face.

That within the great hereafter I may meet them once again,
When my soul has left behind it all this weary pain,
That the pathway still before me I may follow swift and
    brave,
Till I find my past restored me,
O'er the threshold of the grave.


## IF.

### TO J. S. R.

If we had parted then—ah me!
When on that summer day you first beheld me,
Each would have walked, through life, a separate way,
You caring not, whate'er befell me.

If, in that morning's radiance,
When first I saw your manhood's strength and glory.
Your eyes had not sought for my inmost spirit,
And told to me the old-time story.

If God had made you not so true,
If I had lived long years before your being,
Each would have claimed of peace a quiet share,
No dream of happiness believing.

But meeting, heart to kindred heart
Revealed too soon the mutual yearning,
And nevermore can other souls with ours
Thrill in that wild, delicious learning.

Learned *once*, but learned no more,
The truths that bring our lives a blest fruition,
And in the past *we* watch the fading hours
That brought to *us* the sweet transition.


### LINES,
#### SUGGESTED BY READING A POEM BY HECTOR A. STUART.

Oh! for a woman, perfect, pure, and true,
A bard has sung; and pictured her so sweet,
My heart had listened to his magic words,
And worshiped at her feet.

Cruel the power that would a being call,
So fair, so blest, from out her native clime
To wander forth, unmated and alone,
Throughout the bounds of time;

Her white feet wounded, and her pure soul grieved,
To tread the haunts of selfishness and death,
Where woman's fame is lightly held, and oft
Is tarnished by a breath.

Where daughters, loved, and reared with tenderest care
Endowed with every charm of maiden grace,
With mind well stored, with thoughts the most refined,
To crown a beauteous face—

Are, in the glory of their blushing youth,
With soul unspotted as this world has seen,
Yielded at last to grace the proffered home
Owned by some libertine.

So are our hearts' best idols sacrificed,
Life's promise ended in a fate like this;
Their innocence defiled by lips that oft
Have met the wanton's kiss.

O God! thy hand has smote impurity
In the past ages of forgotten years—
Is there no answer to the sad appeal
That speaks in woman's tears?

Must each fond dream of honor fade away,
Our laughter choke in trembling sobs, and must
Precious ideals of truth but crumble down
To very sordid dust?

Oh, for a *man* whose heart is undefiled,
Whose daily acts have made his record fair,
And him our equal—*then* the Bard may dream,
And offer up *his* prayer.

### DISAPPOINTED.

Of my life they were a part,
But I hold them in my heart
　　Only as a memory.
For my bright hopes, one by one,
For their future, all have flown
　　From my life so silently.

Through the strife of many years
Did I toil with patient tears,
    While my young heart earnestly
Beat for them without the stain
Of one selfish wish for gain,
    Beat for them so faithfully.

But the ones so dear to me
Are not what I hoped to see,
    And my heart breaks quietly;
None can see beneath my smile,
How my soul grieves all the while,
    Wounded, oh! so cruelly.

Now the faces loved the best
That were in my faithful breast
    Pictured, oh! so tenderly,
At a deep and bitter cost,
Have their loving interest lost,
    And look up so icily

Into eyes that nevermore,
Till this life of pain is o'er,
    Can look back as happily
As they did in other days,
E'er the cold world and its ways
    Dimmed their light so utterly.


## CONVENT BELLS.

O Convent Bells! whose early chime
    Falls sweetly on the morning air,
You summon, with your brazen rhyme,
    Young hearts to study, blest by prayer.

I pause without the frowning wall,
  Your voices seem a dread decree,
For thus no more, with hallowed call,
  Will Convent Bells ring out for me.

Cursed seem the poor in every clime—
  I heard your summons years ago,
And to the sound my heart beat time
  In glad responses, deep and low.

Since *you* were calling, what to me
  Was work? The wave that bore me on—
I faltered but at fate's decree,
  And now—my early youth is gone.

Glad would I seek the safe retreat
  Where truth and knowledge pure are seen,
Had not the years, with silent feet
  And pallid faces, come between.

Ring out, O Bells! at early morn,
  And let your evening song be sweet,
While one poor heart, bereft, forlorn,
  Finds solace at her Savior's feet.


ONE JULY NIGHT: KLAMATII.

No more in the waning summer,
When over the fading grass,
The first faint sighs of autumn
In trembling whispers pass,

Shall we stand at the evening's threshold
While the harvest moon hangs red
O'er mountains that seemed to listen,
In silence, to all we said.

No more can that magic night-time,
Or the faint and rare perfume
That came from the breath of the roses,
With the river's murmured tune,

Come to us in the mystic glory
Of that hour forever fled,
For the days of that radiant summer,
With its roses, are lying dead.

But that hour, so fraught with feeling,
It lives, like an endless dream
Whose charm has blest, and brought us
A gladness and peace supreme.

When the roses of youth lie faded,
And life's autumn coming on,
With its moaning requiems sighing
Over years forever gone,

We will wait at death's chilling threshold,
While over the hills of Time,
Undimmed in their sacred splendor,
The stars of memory shine.


### AT SAWYER'S BAR.

The summer day was growing late,
   The night-gloom coming on apace,
As leaned a woman o'er her gate,
   With weary, pale, and sin-stamped face.

The record of the many years
   That she had passed in wrong and sin,
Was written, with the trace of tears,
   Where lines of beauty might have been.

Oh! who can read the bitter grief,
   And words that will translate it find,
Of musing o'er her unblest fate,
   By one so cursed by all her kind.

Two ramblers coming down the hill,
   Their white hands filled with roses rare,
Looked on the creature, standing still,
   With face so marked by haunting care.

Her wild eyes seemed to bid them wait,
   Her lips were moved, as though to speak;
She reached her worn hands o'er the gate,
   While tears were trickling down her cheek.

"O, give me one—just one," she said;
   "Not often kindness comes to me;"
And paled her lips, as pale the dead,
   As waked some silent memory.

If ever, in the human face,
   My eyes have read repentance yet,
A *real* regret could there be traced
   Upon those features, blanched and set.

And though the world extends her shame
   Through days that bring her to the grave,
And clogs with vile, dishonored name,
   The soul that *none* have tried to save,

Yet, standing on the last great day
   Before the walls of Paradise,
If she prays Mercy, *thus*, to stay,
   That same wild anguish in her eyes—

That same heart-broken look of woe—
   That same remorse for self and sin—
No angel there will bid her go,
   I think; but surely let her in.

5

## FAITH.

In the gray of the dawn,
When the stars seem at rest,
I shall wait on the hills
That His footsteps have blessed,
For the messenger sent
By a merciful God
To the souls that have tired
Of the paths they have trod.

On the down of his wings
The red light will lay,
That heralds approach,
Of eternity's day;
And reflect on my face,
Till the mark of the tomb
Fades out in the glow
That my features illume.

I know not how soon
I shall wait with the dead
On those hills that have smiled
With that presence long fled;
But His footsteps before
Shall yet guide me to rest,
Through that beautiful dawn
Where our lives are confessed.

From earth, that my spirit
Oft sorely has tried,
To the realm where the blest
In their goodness abide,
My soul, like a flower,
Shall arise from the sod,
To bloom evermore
In the sunlight of God.

## ALAS!

Gone is the dream, and fled the inspiration,
  That to my life I thought would still belong,
Lost is the theme, and lost the sweet vocation,
  And silent now the lips once glad with song.

Quiet the heart that used to beat so fondly,
  And thrill with hopes I never dared to speak,
Roses once red, and passionately burning,
  Faded to ashes on my pallid cheek.

Cold is the heart I learned to love so blindly,
  Wasted the bloom that crowned my early years;
No coming time can touch my life more kindly,
  Nor smooth the traces of my bitter tears.

Now to the portal of a nameless sorrow
  My feet have fled and left the world no trace,
While in the future waits no glad to-morrow,
  Wearing the old-time smiles upon its face.

## AMADOR.

Yet I see thy yellow fields,
As they lay in years before,
Spread beneath an autumn sky,
Fair and fruitful Amador.

In thy canyons and ravines
Miners sought the precious ore,
When I, careless, wandered on,
Through thy pathways, Amador.

But though still thy smiling face
Turns to heaven as before,
Tears are on my own to-day,
As I greet thee, Amador.

Where is now the proud young head,
Yellow as thy golden ore?
In thy dust it lieth low,
And you heed not, Amador.

What are all thy pleasant fields?
What the treasure of thy ore?
Can they bring one pulse of life
To a dead heart, Amador?

Stilled the voice of melody,
I will hear it nevermore;
Silent, like that heart, it lies
Hushed forever, Amador.

Hope once twined the fairest flowers,
Bright the future seemed before;
But they withered and lie dead
On thy bosom, Amador.

Friendship seems an idle name,
But 'twas *real* in times of yore,
When we sang our songs beneath
Thy tamaracks, O Amador!

O'er the waves of Silver Lake,
Or upon its tranquil shore,
Never will our voices blend
In thy moonlight, Amador.

So, while still thy smiling face
Turns to heaven as before,
Tears are on my own to-day,
As I greet thee, Amador.

## TO A LADY.

Some day that waits in coming years,
When our two paths lie far apart,
When Time has marked the careless brow,
And carved his record on the heart,

My smile has faded to a dream,
My presence gone, my words forgot,
My name unspoken, and no voice
To bless by prayer my stranger lot,

Not thinking of the time gone by,
In heedless mood your hand may stray
Toward this book, whose silent leaves
Bear record of a distant day.

Traced by a hand that vanished soon,
Words that had long forgotten lain,
Then from the past so dead and dim,
Call up my absent face again.

And know that though a long "good-by,"
Has slept between us, like a spell
Of silence sad, and left no word
To break that first and last farewell;

That though the merry voice is hushed,
The hand grown nerveless, and the bloom
Chilled into white upon my cheek,
And turned my heart cold in the tomb;

Yet, in a common sisterhood,
We both have known life's pain and joy,
Which makes us kindred, and the years,
*This tie*, at least, can not destroy.

## A REVERIE.

### TO LITTLE ANNIE.

O rest! my darling, rest
Safe on my shelt'ring breast,
  So free from care and pain;
When from my arms you go,
Then never will you know
  Unselfish love again.

I would these tears that fall
Through life were last and all,
  To bathe your worshiped face;
That on your pure, white brow—
Your heart, so guileless now—
  No grief could leave its trace.

Oh! that within my arms,
Safe from all dread alarms,
  My child might ever stay;
Nor learn that woman's fate
Is often desolate—
  Her idols—*only clay*.

Her innocence and trust
Oft humbled to the dust—
  Her worth oft spurned;
When, at unworthy feet,
Her life's devotion sweet
  Is laid, and not returned.

But Time will all too soon
Take back his precious boon,
  And passing silently,
The years will soon depart,
And wean this little heart
  From its great love for me.

But though change Time shall bring,
There is one changeless thing
　　From which will not depart
The love that grows more deep,
When age its vigils keep—
　　*A mother's faithful heart.*


## TO FRIENDSHIP.

This ceaseless march leads surely to the grave,
And friendship's offices are all that save
From deep despair the suffering heart of man,
Who, anguished, works out God's mysterious plan.
So dark does look the portal of the tomb—
So shrinks the spirit from before its gloom;
That hard indeed would be the bed of death,
And filled with moans be every dying breath,
If friendship's voice should fail for dying eyes
To paint the visions of a paradise,
To point the parting soul to its reward,
To vow so faithfully and well to guard,
In solemn promises most true and kind,
The loved and cherished that we leave behind.

When health and beauty bloom upon the cheek,
When eyes are bright, and glad the words we speak,
When sweet Prosperity in shining hours
Has smiled, and strewn our happy way with flowers;
'Tis easy then, as speed our careless days,
To hear the voice that seems sincere in praise,
And oft for favors or for gold we buy
The friends whose flatteries with our fortunes die.
Twice only can we count our friends sincere,
When by our cradle, and beside our bier.

Kind is the heart that does its vigils keep
Unselfishly above our infant sleep;
Still, future years, through hope's fruition fair,
May bring return for all that watchful care;
So, kinder yet, when life's brief day is o'er,
When all its promises delude no more,
When pale the cheek and faint the labored breath,
The one who watches by the bed of death,
And bends above us with a pitying care,
To catch the last sad broken words of prayer
From lips that nevermore may thank or bless
The one who grants this act of tenderness.

To-day we bask in love and love's belief,
Nor deem its day as changing, or as brief;
To-morrow, from it, with unbeating heart,
In long farewell and silently we part,
And those who love us, even in their woe,
May from our open grave be first to go;
While strangers heap between us and the sun
The solemn mound, that tells the end has come.
Kinder than *all* whom we have known and blessed,
The *friend* who gives us to our final rest,
While sorrow fills our place, and looks upon
Those we have left when all our work is done.


## IN THE WATCHES OF THE NIGHT.

While Night, from out her native sky,
Looks down with many a starry eye,
Where all Earth's children seem at rest
Upon their mother's kindly breast;
Why, while the whole world seems to sleep,
Dost thou thy watchful vigils keep,
Astronomer?   What thy reward,
The journeys of the stars to guard?

*I wake*—the dotard and the brute
May lie in sleep enchained and mute;
But writ upon that trackless sky
The fate of ages I descry;    .
*I* can not lose the hours of time
That with such glorious mysteries shine.
*I watch*—that future man may read
The revelations of my creed.

O mother, bending o'er thy child
With heart of love, so true and mild;
Why, till the distant day has dawned,
Do thy petitions pure and fond
Reach to the Author of all light,
Throughout the watches of the night?
And why such ward, unselfish, keep
Above thy baby's peaceful sleep?

Why do I thus, with patience, bear
The task confided to my care?
"*Forbid them not*" (He said), because
Of such his very kingdom was;
And be it peasant, be it king,
A child is still a precious thing;
He holds, if fated to command,
The good of nations in his hand.

And if to humble lot he's born,
I yet will guard him night and morn;
No matter what things *I* endure,
If I can make him wise and pure,
And keep through youth, within his eyes,
The light they brought from Paradise,
The task is grand, in God's great plan,
To rear a *good* and *honest* man.

When thousands lie in rest profound
By slumber's sluggish chain enwound,
With thankless lip, and sin-stamped brow,
For them, O priest! why prayest thou?
" My child, this life is but a span,
Too short to intercede for man;
And, while the sin-fraught ages roll,
I pray for his *undying soul.*"

Up, sluggard! *think* and *watch* and *pray*,
Before *your time* has passed away,
There comes at last unbroken rest,
When rains beat o'er the quiet breast,
Before we hear the sounding horn
That ushers Resurrection's morn—
When life no more is warm and bright,
*Then* sleep through watches of the night.


## WOMAN.

In all the history of the world, *that name*,
In love and honor, has remained the same.
A mediatress she was chosen, when
She interposed between her God and men,
And in her pure arms held in fond embrace
The Infant Savior of our fallen race;
First at the tomb, and last beside the cross,
No plan of mercy can sustain her loss;
Like to the dove, who folds her patient wings,
And mourns her sorrow, yet in mourning sings,
The while her course could reach beyond the stars,
She stays her flight in narrow prison bars,
Far from the world and where its evils lurk,
She fain would turn to seek some chosen work,

Yet shrinks not from the ways of death and sin,
When through their paths a loved one enters in;
She leaves to none, beside her God confessed,
The wrongs that burn in her defenseless breast;
To hands that wound she yet will kiss and cling,
And for the erring her petitions bring,
While tears but fall beneath the chastening rod,
A current bearing her toward her God,
And on that tide which bears *her* surely on,
Have many sinners to forgiveness gone,
That but for prayers and tears so freely given,
Had never passed beyond the gate of heaven.
Without her, *incomplete* this wondrous plan,
This great creation, and its triumph, *man.*


## CENTENNIAL POEM—JULY 4, 1876.

Not to his greatness does my muse aspire,
And yet, like Virgil, I shall sing of arms,
Of strifes and heroes; though the goddess Peace
Has smiled, and banished all of war's alarms.

Here in our first, our fair Centennial's noon,
We meet beneath the glorious Tree of State,
So gather all Columbia's children in,
To-day, with gladness, every heart elate;

Remembering, while its branches spread and hang
Full-fruited through the toil of other years,
The source that gave it life and strength has been
The grand baptism of a Nation's tears.

This freedom that we boast, how was it won?
How made so sure the liberty we claim?
Go read your answer from the scroll of time,
Recorded there, in lines of blood and pain.

Think of the little band of fearless men
Who framed the words that first proclaimed us free;
Who held their hearts within their willing hands,
Their lives an offering for you and me.

Think of the blighted hopes and ruined homes,
The widow's nameless loss, the orphan's tears—
The sowing that no harvest-time could bring,
Till life had ended in the distant years.

Think of our soldiers, who, in want, half-clad,
With weary feet trod through the blood-stained snow,
In patient, suffering, undying hope,
At Valley Forge, one hundred years ago;

Or hearts that broke in British prison hulks,
Where scenes excelled all torments at their worse;
With freedom found but through the gates of death,
Their souls fled, shrinking, from the Hessian's curse.

Go to Mount Vernon, where the pond'rous tomb
That generous heart holds turned to dust;
Whose pulses beat for liberty alone,
Leal to his country and his country's trust;

And ask if ever sentiment was found
Untrue to him, within your traitorous thought;
If so, kneel down in tearful penitence,
O'erwhelmed by all his lifelong service brought;

And thank the Power that gave to *us* the one,
Against whose name the *world* can find no ban,
And blest our country in her darkest hour,
With that most perfect work: *an honest man*.

And since through sacrifice and pain and death
Did we our boon of liberty attain,
Let every true and earnest heart invoke
The ceaseless blessing of her endless reign;

And thank to-day the Providence that kept,
Through that long scourge that came to us but late,
Our rights intact; and made us *one* once more,
Although our sky so long was dark with hate.

For now Peace smiles in gladness from her throne,
There comes no clash of arms, no battle sounds—
Thank God! our land *is free* from dread alarms,
Silent the fife; no bugle-call resounds;

No drummer shrilly beats the fierce tattoo,
Nor sounds the reveille, or long roll's call;
No more in conflict foe with foe shall meet,
While gallant men by kindred hands shall fall.

On southern plains no hostile banner waves,
No cannon's roaring rends the trembling hours,
The track of war has left but heroes' graves
Beneath the tribute of our fairest flowers.

All honor to those *brave* and fallen men,
Whose lives went out for *right* or *erring* cause,
Borne by the roll of drums and bugle's wail,
*Where comes no war, to blanch a nation's laws.*

Though many hearts have said good-by to hope,
When marched their best, away from sight and life,
And homes have lost their darlings, age its stay,
God grant we may *forget* the bitter strife.

Since sin into this glorious, perfect world
First entered through the gates of Paradise,
God, in his wisdom, no boon has given
To man, unheralded by sacrifice.

Ages ago in agony there hung
Upon the cross on Calvary's dark crest,
A Savior dying for a world of sin,
The blood slow trickling from his sacred breast;

With sounds of mourning all the world was full;
For, as those drops touched earth, her great heart broke;
All nature trembled, and in anguished pain,
The sun grew dark, the rocks and mountains spoke,

And as that life so pure—a God's—went out,
It oped a refuge through his sacred tomb,
And by that narrow track, the hosts of sin
Alone have found a sure escape from doom.

So, then, *forget not,* that though pain and death
Our fetters broke, when freedom was begun;
Yet God, to rend the chains of vice and sin,
Gave to the sacrifice *His only Son.*

And since, o'er graves of all our best and great,
Have we strode onward to this time of peace;
Perchance, throughout our land in His good time,
All cruel wrong and bitter strife may cease.

Of all the lands that smile beneath the sun,
Our own most blest; her banner waves afar,
From tropic heat to arctic seas of ice,
Shines out the radiance of Columbia's star.

Our ships of commerce ply from shore to shore,
And bear our products o'er earth's farthest main,
And nations gaze with envious, startled eyes,
Upon the limits of our wide domain.

The wearied slaves of cruel foreign rule
Fly to the refuge that our shores afford,
And bless the country where they find indeed
Manhood their own, and manhood's rights restored.

Cursed be the laws that keep a cringing slave,
That being born in image of his God,
Which warp and bind man's proud, ambitious will,
Subservient to the tyrant's petty rod.

Sons of America, prize full well
The liberty that is your boast and pride;
Sacredly keep the great inheritance
For which our fathers' fathers fought and died.

Within the precious city of our hope
Guard well the watchtowers, and the *entrance gate*,
That ruthless hands may not defile her worth,
Or traitors change the tendence of her fate;

That when, within the lapse of changing years,
Another centenary greets the hours,
Its horoscope may all be written fair,
While not one cloud above its brightness lowers;

While we, long since, have journeyed safely on
Toward the promised, smiling after-lands,
Where, with the authors of our liberty,
We hope to greet, with eager hearts and hands.

## MAY-DAY IN MENDOCINO.

### I.

April, once more surprised by smiling May,
In her fair arms has wept herself away;
Onward she speeds, another clime to seek,
Leaving her tears upon her sister's cheek.
Over the fields the verdant pathways spread,
Tell where the Spring has gone with gentle tread;
We at her shrine with thankful hearts appear,
Laden with flowers of another year;
With no sweeter tribute could we her adore
Than the blossoms lavished from her beauteous store.

### II.

Here the little children come with laugh and song,
Come to gather May-flowers all the whole day long,

And each mother, looking, o'er the radiant sod,
Praying for her darlings, lifts her soul to God,
Asking that the roses still may keep their bloom,
Though the way they border leads but to the tomb,
Saying: "Through the future—through all coming
    morns—
Give to *us* the trials, save *them* from the thorns;"
Till through paths of honor willing feet have made,
Go the little travelers where no blossoms fade.

### III.

Here the youths and maidens seek each wildwood gem,
Fair the world is seeming, crowned with hope for them—
Is it always roses that the young men seek?
Yes, but they are blooming on some maiden's cheek;
Sweet the charms, and many, that the spring adorns,
Full of happy bird-songs, full of golden morns;
But I tell you truly, that the gladdest time
Is when young affection first is in its prime;
Sad it is that ever Time should steal away
All the happy dreaming, blessing it to-day;
Sad that disappointment should with bitter tears
Dim the bright eyes watching for the coming years.
Could we *buy* the freshness only youth can hold,
How would every miser squander forth his gold;
And no gloomy weather would our hearts o'ercast
If the spring of life-time could but only last.
Then go forth and gather in the world your part,
Take some modest blossom, wear it on your heart;
Do not let it languish for the lack of care,
It is yours to cherish.   Keep it always fair.

### IV.

Many to-day, with heads as white as snow,
Dream of the Mays that blest the long ago,

Though in their hearts sweet memory shall sing,
When earth puts on the garb of early spring,
Still, not again can time to them restore
The faces hidden in the great no more.
Oh! where are they—the joys that, known and lost,
Make up the sum of living's bitter cost?
The fair, sweet face, the dear companionship,
The winning smile that wreathed the tender lip,
The child you held so close upon your breast
When death, relentless, called it to its rest,
The loving presence, and the clinging hand,
That beckons now toward the unknown land,
The bright eye's luster, and familiar voice?
When mourning these, the heart can not rejoice;
A sweet reflection from these glad young eyes
May shine like rainbows over wintry skies;
But May has left, for them, her wealth of bloom
Along some path that ended in the tomb.

### v.

But though our own fond hopes be sadly o'er,
Though life's fair spring-time it can come no more,
We hear, while e'er we wander o'er the sod,
A thankful voice that sings its praise to God;
Within our soul its grateful numbers speak,
That still the winds of heaven kiss our cheek;
For charms that still belong to every spring;
For flowers that blow, and happy birds that sing;
Praise it returns, and praising still, is blest,
Though lone it goes toward its final rest.

### VI.

Here in the valley of our favored choice,
Well may we all with laugh and song rejoice,
Far from tearful want, and the blighting drouth,

Over our sisters fainting in the south,
Fields where but late the fruitful seed was sown,
Promise us soon a plenteous harvest-home;
Our redwood forests wave their noble crest
O'er rivers flowing on toward the west;
Lambs are straying over Mount San Hedrim's slope,
And blessed seems, for us, each future hope.
Looking to the east, in her pride appears
Lake, with her blue eyes filled with happy tears;
Yellow-haired Sonoma, lying in the south,
With the kiss of summer waiting on her mouth;
Humboldt on the north, in her youth divine;
To the west the ocean, with its songs sublime;
Fair Mendocino, of them all the queen,
Smiles upon us sweetly, in her robe of green.

# PREDICTIONS AND APPROBATIONS
# OF THE PRESS.

---

As a poetess of rare merit, as a lecturer second to no woman I have heard speak, as a daughter brave and filial, Miss Anna M. Morrison, of California, is respected and honored all over the Golden State, for talent, modesty, and worth. Her future promise is that of winning a proud position on the hill of fame and fortune.—*Correspondence of the New York Weekly.*

CALIFORNIA LITERATURE.—At the request of a number of well-known gentlemen, Mrs. Anna M. Reed, of Ukiah, Mendocino county, formerly Miss Anna Morrison, of Butte county, will issue during the holidays, or soon thereafter, a volume of poems, several of which from time to time we have been pleased to publish in the *Examiner.* While Miss Morrison, the young lady had recourse to lecturing for the purpose of obtaining means to assist in supporting her father's family, and to complete her own education. As a lecturess she was an eminent success, the journals of the different places where she delivered her discourses declaring her to be brilliant and entertaining. As a poetess, we are confident she will prove to be successful, such of her productions in that direction as have come under our observation being possessed of decided merit.—*San Francisco Examiner.*

During the holidays, or soon after, Mrs. Anna M. Reed, *née* Miss Morrison, of Ukiah, will, at the request of nearly one hundred of the leading literary men of the State, publish a volume of her poems. Some years ago, when Mrs. Reed was struggling in the lecture field to assist her father's family, and to secure means to complete her education, the *Golden Era* said of her: "We regard Miss Morrison as the most promising poetical genius of this coast, and, if her prose is equal to her verse, she will gain fame as a lecturer." We shall look earnestly for the coming of Mrs. Reed's volume.—*Golden Era.*

Mrs. Anna M. Reed (Miss Morrison), of Ukiah, Mendocino county, California, will issue, about the holidays, a volume of her own poems. We have had the pleasure of reading many beautiful little gems from the pen of Anna Morrison, and it is with pleasure we learn that we will soon have the little stray leaves put into a neat book. The price of the book will be three dollars, and we have no doubt her thousands of admirers in California will try to secure the volume.—*Santa Ana Herald.*

Miss Morrison, who is a California lady, has written a number of exquisite poetical contributions for the *Golden Era* of this city.—*Figaro.*

A VOLUME WORTH HAVING.—Mrs. Anna M. Reed, the author here referred to, will be remembered by the people of Humboldt as the talented and eloquent young lady who, in 1872, paid a visit to this section of the State in the capacity of a lecturess—then Anna M. Morrison. At that time she was a poor girl, having only the help of her own intellectual endowments, bravely buffeting with the world for the means with which to support the family of her aged father and complete her own education. Nature had highly favored her, however, in the bestowment of her choicest intellectual gifts, and during those dark days many touching and beautiful poems were born to the world through the inspiration of her pen. And now that brighter days have come, she has been persuaded by friends, both old and new, to collect into one volume those poetical gems of her girlhood, and present them to the public in book form.—*Arcata Leader.*

Anna M. Morrison is a name of which California will one day be proud; for she has ability, energy, high purpose, and purity of mind and heart, which will win success. She has written much for the papers, and has attracted the attention and praise of many of the literary men of the coast.—*Grass Valley Union.*

Miss Morrison has had recourse to lecturing for the purpose of obtaining means to assist in supporting her father's family, and to complete her own education. She is a young lady of talent and commendable ambition. *Yreka Union.*

Miss Morrison met with great success and encouragement during her tour up north, and Shasta was not behind her sister towns in lending generous aid to this noble and self-reliant California girl.—*Shasta Courier.*

We predict for this talented young lady a bright and glorious future.—*Butte Record.*

LECTURE.—Miss Anna M. Morrison, Butte county's young and talented authoress, has been giving a series of lectures at Colusa, Princeton, Red Bluff, and other places in Tehama county. She has been highly successful everywhere, and will soon deliver a lecture in Oroville. Her many friends here will be pleased to learn of her success, and to know that her extraordinary talent is employed for the noble and filial object of supporting an invalid father, and a family of young and helpless brothers and sisters. She is a noble girl, and Butte county is proud of her.— *Oroville Record.*

The lecture on Wednesday evening was one of the most brilliant and entertaining ever delivered in our town; and all who heard the lady attest the superior power she possesses as a speaker. Miss Morrison is well aware of the prejudice prevailing against lady lecturers, yet, for the sake of the object she has in view, she is prepared to brave the displeasure of the world. Her aim is a laudable one, and all men should look at the noble girl as she heroically struggles with adversity, and help her on to the consummation of her purpose.—*Chico Enterprise.*

She is the peer of Miss Dickinson in intellect, and of the twain, her lectures will best bear criticism.—*Sacramento Union.*

Mrs. John S. Reed (Miss Anna M. Morrison) is that lady who, for remarkable energy and native talent, has gained a place in the history of California, as one who has been able to stem the current, and keep ahead of circumstances, and make a life compatible to noble ambition.— *Ukiah City Press.*

Mrs. Reed has a fertile imagination, a cultured mind, and a devotion to the muses, which give to her productions a charm and a sweetness which never tire.—*Ukiah Dispatch.*

Without straying from the even tenor of her themes, she weaves around them fancies that show that her imagination is the handmaid of her genius, ever ready to spread the canvas and present the pencil.—*Democratic Dispatch.*

www.ingramcontent.com/pod-product-compliance
Lightning Source LLC
Chambersburg PA
CBHW022342020726
47500CB00004B/1243